This book belongs to

_____

Published by Advance Publishers
© 1998 Disney Enterprises, Inc.
All rights reserved. Printed in the United States.
No part of this book may be reproduced or copied in any form
without the written permission of the copyright owner.

Written by Lisa Ann Marsoli
Illustrated by Adam Devaney and Niall Harding
Produced by Bumpy Slide Books

ISBN: 1-57973-003-5

10 9 8 7 6 5 4 3

DISNEY'S
THE LITTLE MERMAID

TREASURES OF OLD

King Triton's staff was in a flurry. In one week's time, a great banquet would be held in honor of the king's neighbor, King Mariner. Triton had much respect for the old merman, and wished everything to be perfect for his guest. So it was not surprising that the king summoned his trusted court composer Sebastian to help with the preparations.

"Sebastian," King Triton began, "I am especially anxious to introduce King Mariner to my devoted daughters. He only has sons, I'm afraid, and has always longed for a daughter of his own. The least I can do is share their company with him for one evening."

"But of course, Sire," Sebastian replied. "Would you like me to compose something special for the occasion?"

"Not exactly," Triton continued as he and Sebastian swam together. "When the big night arrives, I want all my girls to be on their best behavior — especially Ariel. I'm afraid that, without a mother to guide them, they may not know everything proper young mermaids should. Do you think you can teach them all they need to know in just one week?"

"Just leave it to me, Sire," Sebastian reassured him.

The next day, Sebastian gathered Triton's daughters together and announced a schedule of classes to begin immediately. He also excitedly shared his plans to surprise both kings with a dazzling concert at dinner's end. "Any questions?" Sebastian finished.

"I have one!" called Flounder, who had been watching from the sidelines. "Where's Ariel?"

"Here I am!" she cried, swimming to join her sisters. "I'm sorry, Sebastian, I must have lost track of the time."

Sebastian just shook his head. Everyone knew Ariel was always late — if she remembered to show up at all. "Ariel," he announced grandly, "you're in for a treat. Today's lesson — sit up straight and tall now — posture!"

Ariel just rolled her eyes. She had cut a treasure hunt short for this?

Every day Sebastian tried to teach the young mermaids more good manners. And every day Ariel disrupted the lesson.

For example, during the class on polite dinner conversation, Ariel pretended she had the hiccups and made her sisters howl with laughter.

But every time King Triton asked Sebastian how the lessons were coming, the crab just smiled a great big smile and said, "Splendid, Sire! Just splendid!"

One day Ariel didn't go to class at all. Instead she and Flounder decided to go for a treasure hunt at their favorite shipwreck.

"Won't Sebastian be angry with you?" Flounder asked.

"He's probably happy I'm not there to distract my sisters," Ariel giggled. "Besides, what's so important about this silly old banquet, anyway?"

"Well, it seems important to your dad," Flounder replied. "Maybe you'll even have a good time."

"I doubt it," Ariel told him. "I'm sure the king's very nice, but he's so old. What would I have in common with him? He and my father will have a great time while my sisters and I try not to fall asleep."

Just then Flounder happened upon an interesting-looking trinket in the galley, and the banquet was soon forgotten.

The banquet was still far from Ariel's mind
when the big night arrived.
"I've been looking all over for you!" Sebastian

exclaimed when he found her. "King Mariner will be arriving any minute. Hurry! Go get ready and join your sisters in the dining hall at once!"

Ariel raced back to the palace, combed her hair, and put on her best seashell bracelet. She hurried to the dining hall and saw that she was the last one to arrive.

The only empty seat was beside King Mariner.
As their guest pulled out Ariel's chair, King Triton
shot her a disapproving look. Secretly, though, he
was relieved. At least Sebastian had managed to
round her up this time!

The Little Mermaid sat up straight in her chair. She smiled politely as the food was served. Since she hadn't paid much attention at Sebastian's classes, she wasn't sure what she should do. She watched her sisters and tried her best to copy them. She waited until everyone was served to begin eating.

When King Mariner began to speak, she tried
to look as interested as she could.

But soon Ariel realized she didn't have to pretend to be interested. The old man was full of fascinating stories, and one tale in particular held

the Little Mermaid spellbound.
   It seemed that once upon a time, a pirate ship had sunk right in the middle of Mariner's kingdom!

"We made a record of what was inside it for generations to come," King Mariner told his rapt audience. Then the old man reached into a pocket and brought out a large document.

"Please, no more talk of fish-eaters!" King Triton said with alarm.

But it was too late. The document was already unfurled, revealing detailed drawings of human belongings both strange and familiar. "Wow!" exclaimed Ariel. "There's a snarfblatt!"

"You know what these things are called?" asked King Mariner in surprise.

King Triton looked upset. "I'm sorry to say that my daughter has a fascination with the human world," he explained.

"What a coincidence!" King Mariner exclaimed.
"I do, too! So you can imagine my excitement when
I had a chance to study their artifacts up close."

Ariel and her sisters pored over the sketches. Though King Triton was uncomfortable with all this talk of the human world, he kept silent. After all, King Mariner was his guest. Still, he hoped tonight's tales would not stir his youngest daughter's imagination.

He had a hard enough time keeping her away from the surface as it was!

"What happened to the sunken ship?" the Little Mermaid asked.

"Eventually, what was left of the ship broke apart and drifted away," King Mariner explained.

"And what became of what was inside the ship?" asked Ariel hopefully.

"The objects were of no use to us, so after I was done making a study of them, I let most go where the tides would take them," the old man continued.

"You said 'most,'" the Little Mermaid continued, her spirits rising. "What happened to the others?"

"Funny you should ask," Mariner said with a twinkle in his eye. He reached under the table and brought out an elaborately carved coral box.

The Little Mermaid's sisters got up from their chairs and crowded in closer. Now they were almost as curious as Ariel.

King Mariner turned to Triton as he lifted the lid and brought out seven beautiful necklaces.
"It would be an honor if you would accept these gifts for your daughters," he said.

Triton nodded graciously as his daughters stared
in wonder at the sparkling jewels.

Ariel could not believe her good fortune. That night, as she said farewell to Sebastian and Flounder, she told them what a wonderful evening she had had. "Why didn't you tell me King Mariner knew so much about humans?" she asked Sebastian. "He's so interesting!"

"I didn't know," Sebastian replied. "It just goes to show you — life can be full of surprises!"

"A stuffy party! Oh, how boring!"
Thought the Little Mermaid.
"Ten minutes with that dear old king
And I'm sure I'll be snoring!"
But much to her surprise,
She couldn't tear herself away,
Because both young and old
Have something interesting to say.